PRINCE FROG FACE

PRINCE FROG FACE

Kaye Umansky

With illustrations by
Ben Whitehouse

Barrington Stoke

For Mo and Ella

First published in 2015 in Great Britain by
Barrington Stoke Ltd
18 Walker Street, Edinburgh, EH3 7LP

www.barringtonstoke.co.uk

Text © 2015 Kaye Umansky
Illustrations © 2015 Ben Whitehouse

The moral right of Kaye Umansky and Ben Whitehouse to
be identified as the author and illustrator of this work has
been asserted in accordance with the Copyright, Designs and
Patents Act, 1988

A CIP catalogue record for this book is available
from the British Library upon request

ISBN: 978-1-78112-443-7

Printed in China by Leo

Contents

Chapter 1
How It Began

It all kicked off on a Monday.

I'm talking about the grim business of me getting turned into a frog. I'll tell you about it, but if you dare to laugh, I'll jolly well have you clapped into a dungeon. I can do that because I'm a prince. Prince Valentine of Romantica. With a name like that, I can do what I jolly well like.

Anyway, that Monday I was strolling around the palace gardens because I needed a breather. I had spent all morning interviewing princesses for the top job of being My Girlfriend. Mummy and Daddy think I spend too much time on my hobbies. They say I should get out more. So I agreed to give the girlfriend thing a go. To see if there was anyone up to my standards.

I was wearing my best gold crown, my gold suit and a new pair of gold shoes. I have to say I looked pretty amazing. Blingtastic, in fact. Apart from the pimple on my nose, but I couldn't help that.

There were quite a few princesses up for the girlfriend job. That's no surprise. What's a princess without a prince to prop her up? Nothing, right? And who wouldn't want to be seen with me, with the whole top-to-toe gold thing I had going on?

So far, I had seen six princesses. Six interviews on a Monday morning. I ask you.

None of them were any good. No class at all. Terrible shoes. Too stuck-up or too giggly. They chattered like fools, or they just sat in silence and stared at the pimple on my nose. So rude.

I'd asked them each 20 questions, given them points for their answers and written notes in my little black book. But, to tell you the truth, I was wasting my time. I dismissed them all and told them I'd let them know in the unlikely event that they made the shortlist. They looked pretty fed up as they drove off in their stretch limos. One or two of them were crying into their phones. Sob stories. I wasn't bothered. Plenty more where they came from.

There was the next six, for starters.

Right now, they were out on the terrace taking tea. On my bill, I might add. I'd need to get the money back from them for that later. Footmen were handing around plates of chocolate cake, but none of it got eaten. I suppose the princesses didn't want to spoil their outfits with crumbs. Plus, they were all too busy tossing their hair and being snooty and staring daggers at each other. Well, they were fighting for me, weren't they? They weren't there to make friends. These interviews were a serious business.

So, there I was, taking a breather, when I saw something out of the corner of my eye.

Someone was over by the pond. Bending over, picking something. Not a gardener, or one of the footmen – they don't tend to hang out by ponds. Not a lost princess either, if the rags she was wearing were anything to go by. I looked again. It was a scruffy old woman, dressed all in black and with a basket on her arm.

Chapter 2
Not a Pleasant Sight

A trespasser!

That scruffy old woman was a trespasser.

There's a jolly big notice on the palace gate.

PRIVATE PROPERTY.
TRESPASSERS WILL BE PROSECUTED.

That's what it says. There is also an intercom, to keep undesirables well away.

I'm a prince, see. I don't want any old riff-raff cluttering up the place. Anyone they catch loitering around *my* pad is up for a jolly hefty fine. If they can't pay, then they can spend a night in the dungeon. And that includes old women. They might look harmless, but you can't be too careful.

"I say!" I shouted. I nearly tripped over my shoes in my haste as I marched over. "What do you think you're doing, old woman?"

She stood up and looked me in the eye. She had tangled grey hair and a hooked nose. Hardly any teeth. Compared to even the worst frump of a princess, she wasn't a pleasant sight on a Monday morning.

"Less of the *old*, sonny jim," she said. "Who might you be?"

"Not Jim, that's for sure," I snapped. "I am Prince Valentine. That's a crown on my head. Can't you see?"

"Nope," she said. "I'm blinded by that pimple on your nose. I got some home-made herbal cream that can fix that."

"I don't want your filthy cream," I said. "I asked what it is that you think you're doing."

"What does it look like?" she said. "I'm picking sweezle weed for me potions. Always grows by water, sweezle weed. Matter of fact, I use it in the pimple cream."

She nodded at her basket, which was full of foul, muddy weeds. Nobody would have wanted them, however bad their pimples. But that wasn't the point. They were *my* foul, muddy weeds, and this old hag was stealing them.

"Can't you read?" I said. "There's a notice on the gates. There's an intercom system. This is private property."

"Oh, I don't take no notice of *notices*," she said. She put down the basket and folded her arms. "Mrs Sagacity's my name. I'm a wise woman, see. Some say I'm a witch, but that's their word, not mine. I go where I like, me. Notices don't apply to me."

"Oh yes they jolly well do," I said. "Wise woman or witch. I don't care *what* you are."

Mrs Sagacity stared at me with her beady black eyes. I felt a bit uneasy at what I saw there. Something sinister. A bit scary.

"No, really," she said. "They *jolly* well don't."

I was flabbergasted. I'm a *prince*, right? Nobody argues with me. I was just about to give her a piece of my mind, when she pointed a bony finger up at the terrace.

"Looks like a funny kind of tea party," she said. "What's all them dolled-up girlies doing there?"

"I'm holding interviews," I said. "First round today, if you must know."

"Interviews? For what?" she asked.

"To be My Girlfriend," I told her. "Not that it's any of your business."

"Hmm," she muttered. "You've got a fair old number to pick from there. How are you going to choose?"

"I have a system," I told her. "Points. I score them out of ten."

"Points?" she repeated. "Points for what?"

"Well – having nice shoes, for one thing."

She stared at me. "So. Let me guess. Dainty glass slippers score ten, right? And it would be a zero for – what – clod-hopping brown lace-ups?"

"Indeed," I said. I made a point of staring at her cracked and muddy old boots. I'd give those minus 50, if I was being kind.

"What else do they get points for?" she asked.

"Lots of things," I said. "Whether they're interested in collecting royal mugs."

"That's a hobby of yours, is it?" she said. "Collecting mugs?"

"Yes. And I make scale models of palaces with matchsticks."

"Oooh!" she said. "Exciting! Anything else?"

"Well," I said, "I rather enjoy Boffering."

"Boffering?" She looked blank. "What's that when it's at home?"

"It's all the thrill of sword fighting, but without such a high risk of death," I said. "Boffers are padded weapons. Bofferers bash each other in a combat-like manner."

"I doubt you'll get that lot to do that," Mrs Sagacity said, and she nodded at the princesses on the terrace. "Not with them pointy, sparkly shoes on."

"Oh, will you please shut up about shoes," I said. "Anyway, this is really none of your business. The fine for trespassing on my private property and stealing the royal pond weed is three gold coins, and you can pay up right now."

"Hold your horses, sonny," Mrs Sagacity said. "I'd like to get to the bottom of this points system of yours. You reckon it'll make you popular with the girls, do you? If you give 'em points?"

"Points or no points, of course I'm popular with girls," I snapped. "I'm a prince. I live in a palace. I'm wildly rich and handsome and I've got gold shoes. With buckles. What's not to like?"

"That pimple on your nose, for a start," she said. "Kissed any of 'em yet?"

"I … I have not!" Honestly. Talk about personal. "We're still at the first round stage," I explained.

"Well," Mrs Sagacity said, with a chuckle, "I bet none of 'em want to kiss *you*. Not after all that point scoring. That's no way to behave around young ladies."

Now, that made me jolly well mad. Who did this old woman think she was, with her insults and personal remarks? Who was she to tell me how to behave?

"That's it," I said. "You've done it now. That fine is double now, for your insolent talk. Six gold coins. Or a night in the dungeon. That'll teach you."

"Is that so?" Mrs Sagacity said. Her eyes narrowed. "I don't *think* so, young man. If anyone around here needs to learn a lesson, it's you. I don't like your points system. I don't like your snooty attitude. And those gold shoes are a joke. You need to learn that the world doesn't revolve around you."

She pointed a twisted finger at me and muttered something under her breath. And then the world *did* revolve around me. Everything tipped and spun –

And all went green. Not black.

Green.

A jolly nasty shade of green at that.

Chapter 3
Well, Well, Well!

When I came to, I was lying flat on my back in mud.

Mud?

Mud would ruin my lovely gold suit. Absolutely ruin it!

I sat up and looked down. I wasn't wearing my suit. My best gold shoes had vanished too. Instead ...

Oh. Oh *no*! It looked as if the evil old hag had only gone and turned me into a –

Whaaaaaat?

There were clues. Plenty of clues.

Green skin.

Webbed hands and feet.

The fact that I had shrunk small enough to fit into my royal lunch box.

And a dreadful stink of pond weed in my nose.

In a panic, I felt around on top of my head. Thank heavens for small mercies – and it was a *small* mercy. My crown was still there, but it was the size of a thimble, shrunk to fit me.

My new surroundings were the biggest clue of all. Instead of air, I was surrounded by murky water. Every now and then a bubble floated past. There were rocks, and clumps of green pond weed. I thought the hag had cast me into the palace pond but then I saw steep brick sides all around me. High above my head was the round underside of a bucket.

A well! I was a frog and I was in a *well*!

I clambered to my webbed feet. I took two wobbly steps. My new froggy legs didn't want to step forward with my usual impressive stride. These legs were meant for jumping, of course, so I tried out a little leap. I soared up into the water, much higher than I expected. It was rather good, in fact – like flying. But coming down wasn't so great.

I turned upside down, lost my crown and landed on my head with a muddy squelch.

When I got the right way up again, it was to a peal of bubbly giggles. Three girl toads sat on a rock, laughing at me. I knew they were toads, because I've seen pictures of the horrid warty things. I knew they were girls, because two had on tiny little necklaces made of polished pebbles and the third had a silly bow of pond weed around her head. I had no idea what they were doing down a well. Normally, toads don't live underwater. Of course, most toads don't wear jewellery either, so I guess the rules didn't apply to these three.

I don't like being laughed at. I reached for my crown and put it on. I made my face stern and boggled my froggy eyes at them. They needed to know they stood before royalty.

"Nice hat," the smallest toad said. She was the one with the pond-weed bow. She nudged the middle-sized one next to her. "Look at his hat, Tatiana."

So.

They could talk.

Talking girl toads.

Could my day get any worse?

"It's a crown," I informed her. I gave her a cutting look. "Not a hat. Get it right."

"What's a frog need a crown for?" Tatiana asked.

"I am *not* a frog," I snapped. "I am Prince Valentine of Romantica. A vile and wicked witch has cast a spell on me. This unfortunate frog-like state that I am in is only temporary. So mind your manners or I'll have you incarcerated."

"Oooh, get him with his long words," the small one said.

"He thinks he's posh," the biggest one said. "But his fancy ways don't cut no ice down 'ere. Tell 'im, Tina-Louise."

"I will, Tiffany," the small one said. "Your fancy ways don't cut no ice down 'ere, frog. Ain't that right, Tatiana?"

"Right," Tatiana said.

I decided to ignore them. Horrid, stupid, warty girl toads with their boggly eyes. They'd get minus 100 in my princess points system, and that was me being kind.

I looked up through the murky water to the bottom of the bucket. Freedom lay that way. I would swim to the surface, climb up the bucket, then shimmy up the rope to the top. Then I would find the person in charge and demand they take me home to the palace. Mummy and Daddy would arrest the witch and make her turn me back into a prince. Then they would clap her in the dungeon and bang the door shut behind her.

That was the plan.

I got ready for the leap.

"Going up?" Tatiana asked.

"Doors closing," Tina-Louise said. "Ding! Ding!"

"Au revoir, croaker," Tiffany said. I was surprised she spoke French. Perhaps she wasn't so stupid after all.

I tensed my legs, then leaped. I sailed up through the water like I'd been fired from a cannon. I kept on sailing and my head crashed into the bottom of the bucket, slamming my crown down over my eyes. It hurt. Mocking toady laughter bubbled up from below.

I floundered to one side and thrashed my arms about.

My head broke through the surface, and once again I was breathing fresh air! That was a relief. I bobbed around, adjusted the angle of my crown and planned the next stage of my great escape.

The bucket hung right next to me. Now I had to climb up the side of it.

My new froggy skills came to my aid. My webbed hands and feet worked rather like suckers. My strong back legs gave me the boost I needed. In no time at all I reached the rim.

The bucket hung from a rope tied to its handle. I checked the distance, took a deep breath and jumped. My webbed hands grasped the rope. I dangled there for a second, then lifted up my back legs and pushed. Up I went, as smooth and slick as a circus acrobat. Or, indeed, as a frog. The top of the well came into view. I launched myself into the air and landed on the moss-covered wall.

I crouched there for a moment while I got my breath back and congratulated myself on a slick, accident-free performance. But before I could get my bearings ...

Something round and shiny whizzed past. It only just missed my head and fell into the water with a splash.

Seconds later, there came a terrible scream.

"NNNNOOOOOOO!"

I clapped my hands over my head where my ears would have been, if I still had ears, which I didn't. It really was a jolly loud scream. More of a screech, in fact.

A shadow fell over me. I looked up in fear – and looming over me was a huge, pink, screechy face.

Chapter 4
Feeble Froggy

The face belonged to a girl. She had stubby pigtails and a sharp nose. Her rumpled brown dress looked like a sack and her tiara was crooked. Zero points for looks. Her mouth was open in a huge O.

She stared down at me. Her nose screwed up and her face took on a look of extreme dislike.

"Yuck," she said. "A frog. How disgusting."

"No, in fact," I snapped. "You are quite wrong. I happen to be a prince." I tapped my head with my webbed hand. "See the crown? I am Prince Valentine of Romantica. But it seems I have been turned into a frog by a witch."

"Is that so?" the girl sneered. If she was surprised by the fact that I could speak, she didn't show it.

"Yes," I said. "It is."

"And I'm supposed to believe that, am I?" she mocked.

"Yes," I snapped. "And who might you be?"

"Princess Eugenia. My father is King Richard of Tutitchi. This is my well, in my palace, and you're trespassing."

Ah. Tutitchi. The silly little country next door to Romantica. It wasn't a place I'd normally care to visit, with its mountains like molehills, tiny army and third-rate plumbing. But at least I wasn't on the other side of the world.

"Well, it's not my fault I'm here, is it?" I said. I was pretty cross with the stupid girl.

Eugenia leaned in closer and looked me up and down. "Can you swim?" she asked.

"Of course," I said. "I have excellent froggy skills. But right now, I need help. You must send a message to my parents. I need them to come and collect me. While we wait for them, I need a clean, soft towel to dry myself. I don't want to catch a cold. You can't be too careful. I also require a cushion to rest on."

"Bossy, aren't you?" she said. "For a frog."

"I am *not* a frog," I snapped. "Don't you listen? I also require something to eat. Not a morsel has passed my lips since breakfast this morning."

"What did you have?" She grinned. "Flies?"

"No," I snapped. "Toast. With Marmite."

"Yuck," Eugenia said. "Worse than flies."

"Not to me," I said. "And it's my opinion that counts. Look, are you going to help me or not?"

"That depends," Eugenia said. "One good turn deserves another, right? Dive down and fetch up my golden ball and we might be in business."

Ah. A golden ball. So *that's* what had nearly taken my head off.

"I'm not going back in that well again," I said. "I've spent enough time down there this morning."

"Suit yourself," she said, with a toss of her head. "Fetch the ball and I will send a message to your parents, or don't fetch it and stay green and slimy and hoppy for ever."

I didn't have much choice, did I? She was already walking away.

"Wait!" I shouted. "All right! I'll do it."

"Good," she said. "Off you go, frog face. Get that ball! Fetch!"

So I did. I kicked off, jumped into the water and swam down to the bottom of the well. Tatiana, Tina-Louise and Tiffany greeted me with jeers. They were gathered around the golden ball, which was lying next to a clump of pond weed.

"Here he comes again!"

"Nice to see you, your highness!"

"Big bad world up there too much for you?"

"Shut up," I snapped. "Out of my way."

I pushed past them and hopped up to the ball. I spread my froggy arms as wide as they would go and hoisted it up. I couldn't help staggering a bit. Well, it was jolly heavy.

To my horror, the toads saw fit to burst into song. This is how it went.

"Oooh, look at his muscles,
Feeble froggy muscles,
Heave ho and away we go,
Look at his pea-sized muscles."

I ignored them. Rude, warty nobodies.

I won't bore you with how I got out of the well again. It was jolly difficult, I will say that. My arms were wrapped around the ball and my back legs had to do all the work.

But I did it. It took a while, but I made it in the end. I sat gasping on the wall. I was nearly dead on my green webbed feet.

Princess Eugenia was waiting for me. She gave a little whoop and snatched up the ball.

"Great!" she said. "Daddy would have been cross if I'd lost that. He's only just given it to me."

I gave her a sour look. "Glad you're happy," I said. "Now, can you pick me up – *carefully*, please – and take me to your father. He'll know what to do."

Eugenia eyed me.

"Pick you up?" she said. "Not on your life. You're all cold and slimy. Besides, I don't like you. You're too bossy and hoity-toity. Sort yourself out. I'm off to have lunch."

And with that, she skipped away in her rotten brown dress with her rotten golden ball.

I was speechless.

Chapter 5
An Unexpected Fancy

I wasn't going to let her get away with it. I
hopped off after her.

Eugenia ran across a wide green lawn
and up a flight of steps to the palace terrace.
Easy for her. Not so great for me. The wet
grass had only just been cut and nobody had
raked it yet. Soggy grass cuttings stuck to my
webbed feet. It was like wading through green
spaghetti. The terrace steps were high, too. I
was shattered after my adventures in the well,

and I was cream-crackered by the time I made it to the top of those steps.

Then I had a stroke of luck. Eugenia was one of those people who never shut doors behind them. The palace doors stood open and I crawled inside. I was wheezing and panting as if I'd run a marathon.

A corridor stretched before me. It was lined with tall doors on both sides. I'd never have found Eugenia again if it wasn't for the footman who came rushing out of the third door on the left with an empty tray. He didn't notice me as I dodged around his legs. I made it inside just before the door slammed behind him.

Eugenia was sitting at a long table opposite a tiny man with a beard and a crown. Aha. This must be King Richard. "Rich the Titch," as my parents call him. I noticed he was doing the crossword. Well, I wanted a cross word with *him*.

Clumps of wet grass cuttings fell from my feet as I dragged myself up to the table. I was too tired to hop any more. I gave the king's shoe a brisk tap. He looked down.

"Good grief," he said. "There's a frog in here. Did I order that?"

"Excuse *me*," I said, in my coldest voice. "I am *not* a frog. I happen to be a fellow royal. Prince Valentine of Romantica. I have been turned into a frog by a vile old witch and I require your help."

"Ignore him, Daddy," Eugenia said. "He's a total pain."

"Oh, is that right?" I snarled. "I was good enough to fetch your ball up out of the well, wasn't I?"

"Ball?" the king snapped. "What's all this about, Eugenia? Do you know this frog?"

"She does indeed," I said. "She dropped her ball into the well and I swam down to get it for her. She promised to help me in return. Then she took off."

"Is this true, madam?" King Richard demanded. "Did you?"

"Well – yes," Eugenia muttered. "But look at him, Daddy. He's all slimy. He wanted me to pick him up. As if."

"Eugenia," her father said. "What have I told you about keeping your word? We royals have to lead by example."

Eugenia's sulky face turned even sulkier. "I don't have to set an example to frogs," she grumbled.

"I am NOT a frog!" I shouted. "I'm a *prince*! I'm cold, tired and hungry. I'm in need of help and care. You must inform my parents at once! They won't be happy when they hear about this,

I can tell you. They'll declare war on your silly little country!"

"Now, now." King Richard went a bit pale. "Don't let's be hasty." Romantica has a far bigger army than Tutitchi, and he knew it. "We will do all in our power to help," he said. "But first, let's get you something to eat. Eugenia, place the fr– our guest on the table. He will share our lunch."

"But, Daddy –" Eugenia began.

"Do it," the king snapped. "Now."

Eugenia scowled. She leaned down, snatched me up and dumped me on the table. She was none too gentle about it.

"Yuck," she said, as she wiped her hand on her dress. "Gross."

"What would you like, Prince Valentine?" King Richard asked. He waved at the silver platters on the table. "Fruit, eggs, salad? Ham, cheese? Bacon, sausage, beef? Take your pick."

I cast my eyes over the table. There was no Marmite, but it was a good spread. I was starving.

"I'll have a cheese omelette," I said. "And a sausage. Please."

"Excellent choice," the king said. "Eugenia, ring for an extra plate."

"Don't bother," I said to Eugenia. "You seem to have finished. I'll eat off yours."

I knew that would get to her. But she didn't dare say anything, because her father was glaring daggers at her.

"So," King Richard said. "Prince Valentine. How nice of you to join us. Didn't I hear that you're looking for a girlfriend?"

"Yes," I said. It made a change to speak to someone who showed me some respect. "I'm right in the middle of the interview process, as a matter of fact," I told him.

"*You?*" Eugenia hooted. "Frog face! A girlfriend? Whoever's going to want to go out with *you?*"

"Eugenia!" the king snapped. "Manners, if you please. And please be so kind as to serve our guest. He can hardly do it himself, can he?"

Eugenia snatched up a fork and dumped an omelette on her plate, and then a sausage. It was a burnt one. It smelled all charred and sooty.

"Not that one," I said. "One that's rather less burnt, if you please."

With a scowl, Eugenia speared the burnt sausage and replaced it with one that looked a

little better. I had to duck as the lethal prongs of the fork whizzed past my head.

I broke off a corner of the omelette and placed it in my mouth. It didn't taste at all nice. I had an unexpected fancy for a mouthful of crispy mayflies. Oh no! Even my appetite had become frog-like. The sooner I got changed back into a prince the better.

I didn't wish to spoil the tablecloth, and so I spat out the omelette into Eugenia's lap.

"Lovely," she said. "Frog gob. Thanks for **that**."

"Do you know, I find I'm not that hungry after all," I said. I wasn't about to admit to the mayfly thing. "What I need is rest. I feel a little faint."

"Of course," King Richard said. "Eugenia, take the fr– er, Prince Valentine to your

bed chamber and tuck him up. I will send a
message to Romantica right away."

"Oh, but, Daddy –" Eugenia began.

"*Now*, if you please."

Eugenia's face was a picture of outrage.

Good.

Chapter 6
Moan, Moan, Moan!

I didn't see much on the way to Eugenia's bed chamber. That's because she rammed me deep down into the pocket of her dress. It was hot, stuffy and filled with old tissues and sweet wrappers, so I was hardly able to breathe.

When at last we made it to her room, she took me out and threw me onto her frilly duvet. My froggy body made a slimy damp mark where I landed.

We glared at each other with dislike.

"Don't move," she said. "I'll get a towel."

She marched out of the room. When she got back, I had arranged myself on her soft silk pillow. There were little webbed footprints and a scattering of soggy grass all over the duvet. I had done that on purpose.

She spread the towel out and patted it. "Sit on this, frog face," she said. "Look at the mess you've made. Move yourself. I don't want your nasty green body on my pillow."

"Tough," I said. "I'll sit where I want. And stop bossing me around, or I'll jolly well tell your father."

We glowered at each other again.

But then an unexpected voice interrupted our staring match. (I'd been set to win, by the way).

"How's it going then, sonny? Having fun?"

It was Mrs Sagacity! She leaned against the door and smirked, chewing on a stalk of sweezle weed.

"This is one weird day," Eugenia said. "Who might you be?"

"I'm the one what turned him into a frog," Mrs Sagacity explained. "Just popped by to see how he's getting on. I thought I'd see if he's learned how to behave around young ladies."

"Oh, I'm having a wonderful time," I said bitterly. "I've been dumped into filthy water, sneered at by a trio of bad-mannered singing toads, lied to, mistreated by this rude upstart of a girl ..."

"Oh, stop moaning, frog face," Eugenia broke in. "Moan, moan, moan! All you do is moan." She turned to Mrs Sagacity. "I hope you're taking him away, because I've had more than enough of him."

"You don't want to kiss him goodbye, then?" Mrs Sagacity said.

"*Kiss* him?" Eugenia put her finger in her mouth and made gagging noises. She really was *too* coarse. "Bleugh! Ptthuggh!" she cried. "No chance!"

Mrs Sagacity winked. "Not even a little peck on the cheek?"

"No way," Eugenia said. "I'd sooner lick a slug. Uggy-uggy-uggggh!"

"Pity," Mrs Sagacity said. "A kiss from you would break the spell, see. He'd change back into a prince."

"I don't care," Eugenia squealed. "I'm not kissing him. Yuck, the very thought!"

"Course, there's something else that might work," Mrs Sagacity said. "Shock treatment. A sharp bang on the head. Worth a try."

"That sounds more like it," Eugenia said. "My pleasure."

And before I could protest, she picked me up by my froggy back leg and threw me at the wall.

SPLAT!

I slithered down the wall and ended up in a heap on the floor. I tried to stand up.

Once again, the world wobbled and spun around me, and everything went –

Black.

Chapter 7
No Webbed Feet

This time, when I came to, I was back where I started – standing by the side of the royal pond.

To my great relief, I was no longer a frog.

No webbed feet.

No embarrassing hunger for mayflies.

No green and slimy skin.

No stink of pond weed in my nose. I was myself again.

My gold suit wasn't even wet! I patted my head to check for my crown. Yes. Still there. Gold shoes? Ditto. I felt my nose. Sadly the pimple was still there too. I was a bit groggy from where my head had hit the wall, but apart from that I felt ... normal. Normal for a royal prince, that is.

Mrs Sagacity was standing back, looking me over.

"Better?" she said.

"Yes," I said. "No thanks to you."

I looked up at the terrace. It was empty. It was clear that my would-be girlfriends had given up and gone home. Who could blame them? The sun was setting. I must have been away all day.

"So. Now what?" Mrs Sagacity asked.

"I'm going in for dinner," I snapped. "I haven't eaten a thing today."

"So you won't be wanting them gold coins, then?" she said. "The fine for trespassing?"

I looked into her sly eyes. I didn't want to back down, but it wasn't worth the risk.

"No," I said. "I'll let it go this time." And I turned my back and marched away.

"No more daft points system!" she shouted after me. "No more interviews! How about getting to know people before you judge 'em? I can turn you back again, you know!"

I ignored her and marched into the palace. I held my head high and my gold shoes tap-tapped across the terrace.

Chapter 8
No Time for Girls

Dinner was wonderful.

I ate three lamb chops with roast potatoes
and gravy. Yummy. Then I had two helpings
of sticky toffee pudding. With custard. And
cream. There was a bowl of leafy salad, but I
steered clear of that. I didn't fancy anything
green.

Mummy and Daddy could see I was trying
to focus on my dinner, but they kept quizzing
me.

"But where have you *been*, darling?" Mummy asked. "You vanished this morning and we haven't seen you since. We even had the guards search the grounds."

"We had to send the princesses home," Daddy said. "They weren't too pleased, I can tell you. I don't think we'll be sending them any bills for tea and cake now."

"Sorry," I said. "I went for a walk. Sat under a tree. Must have dropped off."

"Well, it was too bad of you," Mummy said. "I don't know who we can drum up for the next round of interviews now. I suppose we could try Princess Eugenia of Tu–"

"No!" I shouted. "Never! Not her!"

They both looked startled.

"All right, son, no need to shout," Daddy said.

"Look," I said. "I don't think I'm in the mood for a girlfriend right now. I'd like to leave it for a while, if it's all the same to you. I've got an important Boffering contest coming up. And a matchstick palace to finish. And I need to catalogue my royal mug collection. You see? No time for girls. So, if you'll excuse me, I'm off to bed."

So that's what I did. I trudged up to my bed chamber. I took off my crown and my gold suit. As I undressed, I wondered whether it had all been a bad dream. Perhaps I had indeed sat down under a tree and gone to sleep. Perhaps Mrs Sagacity hadn't even been real.

Last of all, I took off my gold shoes.

Which were full of pond weed.

I tipped it out the window and went to bed.

Chapter 9
How It Ended

I got over it, of course. But my gold shoes were never the same again. It's nasty stuff, pond weed.

The frog thing had been pretty bad, but time moved on, and at last there came a night when I didn't have watery nightmares. I added three new royal mugs to my collection. I finished the matchstick palace. I lost the Boffering contest, but we won't go into that.

Mummy and Daddy started to drop hints about girlfriends again. They sent off a load more invites to a new batch of princesses to come for an interview.

We had a poor response, I'm afraid. It seems quite a lot of princesses know Eugenia. It turns out they all belong to the same pony club. It was clear that she had been saying bad things about me behind my back. Princesses are like that.

Anyway.

There I was again, sitting at my desk with my little black book in front of me. I had my pen at the ready, about to interview the only princess who had turned up. Her name was Hortense. She was wearing a riding outfit, complete with boots and helmet. She told me she was only here because her riding lesson was called off and she'd heard there was chocolate cake.

I was just about to score her a big fat zero, when something stopped me.

I had seen past Hortense and out the window. There, down by the pond, was an old woman in black. She was pulling clumps of weed from the water and adding them to her brimming basket.

The old woman turned and looked my way.

I snapped my little black book shut as fast as I could.

"So, Hortense," I said. "I take it you're not looking for a prince to sweep you off your feet?"

"No," she said. "Not really. To be honest, I prefer ponies. Mine's called Sugar Lump. That's because he's small and white and the sweetest thing you ever saw."

"Good name," I said. Well, it is.

"Thanks," Hortense said. She sounded pleased. "Do you like ponies?"

"I'm not sure," I said. "I've never tried riding. I'm more into indoor hobbies. Like making model palaces out of matchsticks."

"Really?" she said. "Wow. Sounds fiddly. You must show me some time."

This cheered me up. Not many people are interested.

"I collect royal mugs as well," I told her. "I arrange them in size order on special shelves in my hobby room."

"You have a hobby room?" she said. "Well, good for you!"

I was surprised this was all going so well. I was having a normal, pleasant chat. With a *girl*.

"Have you heard of Boffering, by any chance?" I said. "It's a game where you whack the other player with a special padded weapon. I play it in the corridors with the footmen."

"Sounds fun," Hortense said. "I wouldn't mind having a go at that. If you have go at riding."

"All right," I said. "It's a deal."

"Good-o," Hortense said. "That's settled, then. Come over to my place tomorrow and meet Sugar Lump. So. *Is* there any chocolate cake?"

"Yes," I said. "Loads. And Marmite sandwiches."

"Excellent," she said. "I love Marmite."

We stood up together and headed off to take tea together on the terrace. As we left the room, I glanced out the window. There was Mrs

Sagacity, with her basket of sweezle weed. She grinned and gave me the thumbs-up.

I returned it. Well, you can't be too careful.